Contents

Series Reading Consultant: Prue Goodwin
Lecturer in Literacy and Children's Books, University of Reading

Kingston Library
LIBRARY & HERITAGE S

WWW

Renew a book
Change of
Library news an
Search the c

New
48 Ki
New
KT3

15
12 AP

- 9 JU 20

- 6 DE

Monster
Crisp-Guzzler

MALORIE BLACKMAN

by Sami Sweeten

PUPS

KT 1029036 2

Also available by Malorie Blackman,
and published by Corgi Pups Books:

SNOW DOG
SPACE RACE!

THE MONSTER CRISP-GUZZLER
A CORGI PUPS BOOK : 9780552547833

First publication in Great Britain

PRINTING HISTORY
Corgi Pups edition published 2002

13

Copyright © 2002 by Oneta Malorie Blackman
Illustrations copyright © 2002 by Sami Sweeten

The right of Malorie Blackman to be identified as the author
of this work has been asserted in accordance with the
Copyright, Designs and Patents Act 1988

Condition of Sale
This book is sold subject to the condition that it shall not,
by way of trade or otherwise, be lent, re-sold, hired out or
otherwise circulated without the publisher's consent in any
form of binding or cover other than that in which it is
published and without a similar condition including
this condition being imposed on the subsequent
purchaser.

The Random House Group Limited supports The Forest Stewardship
Council (FSC), the leading international forest certification oranisation.
All our titles that are printed on Greenpeace approved FSC certified paper
carry the FSC logo. Our paper procurement policy can be found at:
www.rbooks.co.uk/environment.

Set in 18/25pt Bembo MT Schoolbook

Corgi Pups Books are published by Random House Children's Books,
61–63 Uxbridge Road, London W5 5SA,
A Random House Group Company

Addresses for companies within The Random House Group Limited
can be found at: www.randomhouse.co.uk/offices.htm

Printed and bound in Great Britain by
Cox & Wyman Ltd, Reading, Berkshire

For Neil and Lizzy, with love.
And for Elizabeth, Eshaa, Francesca,
Katy, Emily, Charlotte, Nicole, Alice,
Sarah, Ellie, Josie, Hannah, Anna,
Lily, Jessica, Jenny, Caitlin, Jodie,
Grace, Holly and Bronte.
And for Hilary Porteous, who
loves crisps!

Chapter One
Miss Porter's Secret

Hi everyone! This is me, Mira Morris. And this is Miss Porter, my teacher. Miss Porter has long black hair which she wears in a French plait down her back, and dark brown eyes which sparkle and fizz when she looks at you.

She looks quite ordinary, doesn't she? BUT SHE'S NOT! Not a bit of it. She has a *secret* – and I know what it is. And if you promise not to tell anyone, I'll tell you too. D'you promise? OK then. This is how I found out Miss Porter's secret.

On my very first day at my
new school, I sat next to Hannah
who was very friendly. Hannah
showed me around the classroom
and told me where everything
was.

"What's Miss Porter like?" I
whispered.

Hannah
looked around.
Miss Porter was
at the other side
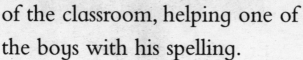
of the classroom, helping one of
the boys with his spelling.

"She's great!" Hannah
replied. "But watch out!

Sometimes she can be a bit of a dragon!"

And for some reason Hannah and Josie and Nicole and all the others around me burst out laughing.

"Er, what's so funny?" Miss Porter called across the classroom.

"Nothing." The laughter stopped at once.

"Back to your tables then," said Miss Porter. "It's nearly break time."

Hannah, Josie, Nicole and I sat at our table just as the mid-morning buzzer sounded.

Yippee! It was time to get out our break-boxes – and I was *starving*! I took out my Betsy Bear break-box, eager to see what Mum had packed for me.

There was a honey sandwich (my favourite sandwich), a blackcurrant drink (my favourite drink!), a few grapes (my favourite fruit) and a packet of salt and vinegar crisps – my

favourite food in the whole, wide world. I opened up the crisp packet first.

"Oh no!" Hannah exclaimed. "You've got crisps!"

"Hide them! Hide them!" Josie urged.

Nicole just  stared at me like I was crazy.

"What's the matter?" I asked.

But I didn't get any further. Something strange was happening at the other side of the classroom. Miss Porter had been putting some books back on the bottom shelf of the bookcase when she suddenly sprang to her feet, her eyes wide and staring.

"Who's got crisps?" she demanded. "Who's got crisps?"

And then her tongue came out to lick her lips. Only it wasn't a normal tongue. It was forked, split in the middle like a snake's tongue and it was at least as long as my whole arm!

Chapter Two
Miss Porter Changes

I blinked. Then blinked again,
sure my eyes were playing tricks
on me. Miss Porter started
sniffing and moving slowly
round the classroom.

Josie tried to snatch my crisps
out of my hand, but I snatched
them back.

"Excuse me!" I said. "If you
want a crisp, ask first!"

"I don't want your crisps, but
the monster crisp-guzzler does,"
Josie told me.

"The *who*?"

"Me!" Miss Porter appeared from nowhere to squat down beside my chair. "It's just a little nick-name my class has for me. They call me the monster crisp-guzzler because I love crisps so much." Miss Porter gave me a great, big beaming smile. And her tongue was back to normal. I shook my head. Had I been imagining things?

"As I don't eat meat, they have to be vegetarian crisps of course," Miss Porter continued.

"What flavour are yours? Salt and vinegar?"

I nodded. "Mum always puts a packet of crisps in my break-box because she knows how much I love them."

"So do I! I love them! I adore them! I want to marry them!" Miss Porter grinned.

"Miss Porter, please don't,"
Nicole pleaded. "You know
what happens every
time you eat crisps."

"Nonsense," Miss
Porter told her. "One
itsy-bitsy-teeny-tiny
little crisp isn't going to hurt."

"But that's the trouble,"
Hannah argued. "You never
have just one itsy-bitsy-teeny-
tiny little crisp."

"Nonsense," Miss Porter
said again. "You all
worry too much."
I still didn't have a clue

what was going on.

"Would you like a crisp, Miss Porter?" I asked doubtfully, holding the bag up for her.

The whole class gasped in horror. It went very quiet as our teacher sniffed at my bag of crisps. She closed her eyes like just the smell alone was enough to take her to Heaven!

I looked around the classroom. Everyone was holding
their breath as they watched
Miss Porter and me.

"Miss Porter, don't do it . . ."
Ellie called from the next table.

"Just one . . . just one . . ."
Miss Porter was practically
drooling over my crisp packet
now.

And all at once I got a very strange, hiccupy feeling in my tummy. I didn't think it was a very good idea to give Miss Porter any of my crisps, but how could I take them back without seeming rude?

"You don't mind if I have one crisp, do you, Mira?" asked Miss Porter.

I shook my head slowly. "No, Miss Porter."

My teacher dipped her hand
into my crisp packet
and took out four or
five crisps together.

"Is that OK?" she
asked.

I nodded.

"I really am
a monster crisp-guzzler, I'm
afraid!" laughed
Miss Porter
and she
popped the
crisps
into
her mouth.

And then it happened. Not just her face but her whole body began to change. She grew crinkly and wrinkly and started sprouting scales all over her arms and her legs and her face. Her ears grew up and her nose grew out and her teeth grew down and enormous wings appeared from nowhere, sprouting out of my

teacher's back. And she had the
longest tail I'd ever seen on any
creature. It curled right round the
classroom and moved

gently up
and down like
a huge,
long
finger
waving.

"Delicious!" She licked her lips. The enormous, forked tongue was back. "Can I have a couple more?"

"I knew it! I just knew it!" said Josie.

I didn't even notice that my packet of crisps had fallen from my hand. I was staring so hard, my eyes were beginning to hurt. Miss Porter wasn't a woman any more. My teacher had turned into . . . a dragon!

Chapter Three
In Trouble

"Mira, we warned you not to give her any crisps," Nicole snapped. "This is what happens every time Miss Porter eats them."

I didn't know whether to
scream or burst out laughing.
I couldn't have been more
shocked if I'd been thrown into
a swimming pool full of ice-cubes.

"I . . . I haven't changed, have
I class?" asked Miss Porter.

"YES!" everyone shouted back.

"Oh dear! Oh dear!" Miss Porter said, her huge wings fluttering behind her. "I only had a few."

Barry, one of the boys at the front of the class, ran to the door. He opened it slightly and peered out.

"It's OK. The corridor is empty – so far," he said with relief.

"I'm sorry. I didn't know," I gasped, still staring at Miss Porter. "Someone should've warned me."

"We tried," Nicole said, shaking her head.

I pulled my chair away from Miss Porter, the dragon. I hardly dared to breathe. She said she was a vegetarian but suppose that was only when she was a teacher? Suppose when she was a dragon she turned into a . . . girl-eater?

"It's OK, Mira. I'm not going to hurt you, I promise," Miss Porter told me. "I can't help being a dragon!"

"You wouldn't be one if you could stop eating crisps," Hannah pointed out.

"H-h-how long are you going to stay a dragon, Miss Porter?" I asked.

Miss Porter shrugged her dragon shoulders. "No idea. It might just be five minutes. It might be five hours. I have no way of knowing."

"Quick, Miss Porter! Hide! The headmistress is coming!" yelped Barry from the door.

 I picked up my crisps and shoved the packet back into my breakbox. They'd done enough damage for one day.

"Oh dear! If Mrs Sprat catches me like this, she'll sack me, for sure," Miss Porter wrung her scaly paws in alarm and looked around desperately for somewhere to hide.

Barry hurried back to his
desk, only just in time. The door
was flung open. And there stood
Mrs Sprat. She looked around,
her eyes narrowing
suspiciously.
"Where's Miss
Porter?" she
asked no-one in
particular.
"Er . . . she just
stepped out for
a moment,"
Hannah replied.

"Stepped out where?" asked
the headmistress.

34

"She didn't say," Hannah
rushed on. "Sorry."

I had to fight to look at Mrs
Sprat and not at what was
going on above her. Miss Porter

was floating right above her
head, her long tail wrapped
around her body in coils.

She placed one finger over her scaly lips as she signalled to us not to give the game away.

"Well, she shouldn't leave you alone. I'll go and find her immediately. If she comes back, could one of you tell her I'd like to have a word with her," said Mrs Sprat.

We all nodded our heads vigorously. Mrs Sprat left the classroom.

Miss Porter floated down from above the door, her tail uncurling. I wiped the perspiration off my forehead in relief. And I wasn't the only one. That'd been too close! I'd thought Miss Porter was in trouble for sure.

"Thanks for not giving the game away, class," Miss Porter began. "I really thought that . . ."

"Oh, class, could you tell . . ." Mrs Sprat entered the room and stared at Miss Porter the dragon.

I held my breath. What was going to happen now? I expected Mrs Sprat to run screaming from the class. But she stood there, looking more and more cross.

"Miss Porter, I warned you what would happen if you turned into a dragon in my school again," said Mrs Sprat, her eyes shooting sparks. "You will work till the end of this week until I can find someone to replace you. After that you will no longer be welcome at my school. You're dismissed!"

Mrs Sprat slammed out of the classroom. We all stared in horror. Just like that, Miss Porter had lost her job. And I felt worse than anyone, because it was all my fault.

Chapter Four
The Rescue

The rest of the week flew by
and we didn't want it to. Even
the prospect of a school trip to
Ramsden Bay by the seaside on
Friday couldn't cheer us up.

Everyone was very aware that
Friday was going to be our last
day with Miss Porter.

We got a surprise when we all climbed into the coach on Friday morning. Mrs Sprat, the headmistress, was our driver.

"I've decided to come with you to make sure that none of you," she turned to glare at Miss Porter as she said it, "none of you gets up to any mischief!" And with that we set off.

When we got to Ramsden Bay, the beach was warm and sandy and the sea was a deep bluey-green and the weather was lovely. We were the only ones for kilometres, it couldn't have been more perfect.

But I wasn't the only one moping around.

"Cheer up, class." Miss Porter tried her best to make us smile. She pulled silly faces and tried to juggle with some shells and seaweed. We did laugh, especially when a long, smelly piece of seaweed fell on Miss Porter's head — but it didn't last long. This was our very last day with our teacher.

I'd only been at the school for a week but I already knew that Miss Porter was something special. She was patient and kind and a really good teacher. I was going to miss her.

"If only there was something we could do to change Mrs Sprat's mind," I said to my new friends.  They all just sighed and nodded their heads. We walked along the beach looking into rock pools and watching the crabs and starfish.

We ate our lunch and made
sand castles and bought gifts in

the gift shop, until all too soon it
was time to go home. Back in
the coach, I looked around for
my lunch-box.

"Oh no!" I exclaimed. "Miss
Porter, I've left my Betsy Bear
lunch-box over by
the last rock pool
we were studying."

"Really, Mira! Why on earth did you put it down?" asked Miss Porter.

"I wanted to hold a starfish and I was afraid it might fall out of my hands if I was holding on to my box as well," I explained.

"I can see the rock pool from here. Can I go and get it please?"

"Hurry up, then," said Miss Porter. "Go straight there and come straight back."

As I got out of the coach, I
could see the white, foamy crest
of the sea breaking on the beach.
I ran all the way to the rock pool
where I'd left my box. But it
wasn't there. In the distance, I
could see a big seagull, dragging
it along the beach.

"That's mine," I cried out, and started running after it.

The seagull took off with a "Crawww! Crawww!", leaving my box behind. When at last I reached it, I picked it up and dusted off the sand. I turned around – and screamed.

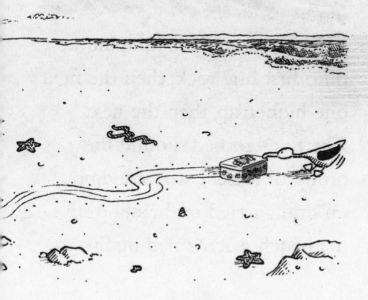

The tide, which had seemed so gentle and far away before, was now racing up the beach like a galloping horse. And it was only a few metres away.

I turned and *ran*, jumping up onto first one rock, then the next one higher up, then the next. The tide crashed around the group of rocks I was standing on and carried on heading up the beach. I screamed again.

All around me the water was
getting higher and higher.

In the distance I could see
some of my classmates pointing
at me from the coach. Miss
Porter jumped out of the coach
and came racing towards me.

Mrs Sprat and all the others poured out of the coach and sprinted behind her.

"Help! Someone, help!" I yelled.

Miss Porter looked around, frantically searching for some-one or something to help us.

But apart from our school party
we were alone. And the tide had
come in so quickly, Miss Porter
and I were too far apart for her
to grab me.

"I'll get her.' Mrs
Sprat pulled off
her jacket and
kicked off
her shoes.

Miss Porter
pulled her back.
"The tide is too
fast and the current is too
strong. You'd be swept away
before you ever reached her."

"Do something! Help!" I screamed. The water was lashing higher up the rocks. "Does anyone have any crisps?" Miss Porter called out suddenly.

"No." Everyone shook their heads.

"I'll get you some," Mrs Sprat said, determination on her face.

She lifted up her long, flowery skirt and sprinted down the

beach towards the gift shop. And
all the time the sea water
around me was rising
and rising.

Only a
couple more
centimetres and
then it would

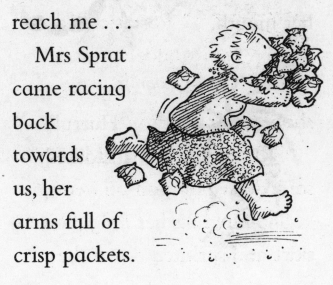

reach me . . .

Mrs Sprat
came racing
back
towards
us, her
arms full of
crisp packets.

When the headmistress reached
her, Miss Porter grabbed the
nearest packet and tore it open.
Tilting her head back, she put
the packet of crisps to her lips
and let the
crisps
fall into
her mouth.

"Hurry!"
I shouted.

The sea charged against the rocks I was standing on, spraying up onto my socks and skirt. One more centimetre and it would reach the soles of my sandals. But as I watched, Miss Porter's shoulders began to heave up and down. She rubbed her growing nose. Wings sprouted out of her back. The longest tail of any animal anywhere began to whip up and down behind her.

"Quick!" I yelled.

Wasting no more time, Miss
Porter flew over to me and
lowered her tail.

"Mira, grab hold.
Quick!" she said.

She didn't need
to tell me twice. I
jumped up and
grabbed hold of
her tail. And
only just in
time too. The
tide crashed over the
rocks where I'd been standing
only a second before. I held on
tight as we flew over the sea.

Miss Porter's tail was very
warm but scaly and rough –
which was just as well because
if it'd been smooth, I would've
slid right off it into the sea
below. We were
flying so fast, the
wind whipped
over my face
and through my hair.

I could see for kilometres as Miss Porter flew further up the beach to where it was safe. She made sure my feet were on the ground before she landed herself.

"Hooray for Miss Porter!" the class cheered.

"Oh, it was nothing really." Miss Porter the dragon looked happy and embarrassed at the same time.

"Mrs Sprat, wasn't Miss Porter wonderful?" asked Hannah hopefully.

"Yes, she was." Mrs Sprat smiled at Hannah before turning to Miss Porter. "Perhaps I was rather too hasty in telling you to leave. You may have your job back, but only if you behave yourself! No more turning into a dragon during school hours. No more crisps. Promise?"

"I promise . . ." said Miss Porter, adding under her breath, "I promise I'll try!"

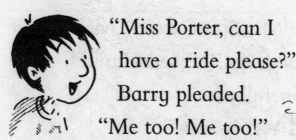

"Miss Porter, can I have a ride please?" Barry pleaded. "Me too! Me too!"

"Er, I don't think Mrs Sprat would be too happy about that," said Miss Porter.

"We've got about thirty minutes before we have to set off, so why not?" Mrs Sprat surprised us all by saying.

Miss Porter gave everyone in the class a ride on her back, over the sea and along the beach until the crisps wore off and she turned back into our teacher.

By the time we got back to the coach, we'd all had the most wonderful time, ever. We got back onto the coach and sang songs all the way home.

Even Mrs Sprat joined in. It was terrific. I didn't mind getting wet if it meant Miss Porter could still be our teacher. Miss Porter had a secret that only the others in my class and the headmistress knew, and that was the way it was going to stay.

So just think! All that happened in my first week at school. I can't wait for next week!

THE END